THE TREE
of DREAMS

Written by David Greygoose
Illustrated by Jane Tattersfield

Collins Educational
An imprint of HarperCollinsPublishers

The tall Tree stood at the heart of the wood and gazed out to the hills and the streams.

The Tree stood strong, and its branches stretched like arms, cradling blackbirds and thrushes, linnets and robins, tiny crawling spiders and clambering squirrels in its gnarled and knotty hands.

In the warmth of its shadow crept beetles, mice and snails, travelling their worlds each turning day.

And when the high sun shone, the Tree waited patiently, watching as the people came out from the town: out through the gates across the patchwork of fields where slow sheep grazed and cattle lowed beside the whispering corn.

Mothers and children, fathers and brothers, babes-in-arms, grandparents, sisters and lovers would come to the Tree on a fine afternoon and stay there until the rise of the moon to tell the old stories each learnt from another, while the Tree smiled and listened till each dancing leaf was a map charged with wisdom, and its bark engrained with tales and memories.

Then one by one they would make their way home, laughing and singing the new strength they shared with the tall Tree which stood at the heart of the wood, gazing out to the hills and the streams; the tall Tree that called them and held them and knew them; the Tree they all trusted: the Tree of Dreams.

And then without warning, out of the sun, the White Worm came – a huge winged serpent swooping low over the roofs of the town that nestled behind the walls, beneath the hills, outside the wood.

The White Worm came. It came without a sound, without a reason, without a name – the White Worm came. At night its wings beat silence above the sleeping people, scratching for silver, trawling for gold, slavering for food at each double-locked door; pilfering sweet secrets, stealing precious dreams, replacing trust and friendship with emptiness and fear. And at dawn, as its shadow snaked through the sky, its breath scorched the fields as it flew to the wood and coiled its scaly body around the Tree of Dreams.

Beneath the Tree it buried its lust for stolen gold. And from the Tree it sucked every dream that had been told.

2

3

4

Now there is no harvest,
Now there is no food,
As the White Worm winds through the silent wood
Dragging gossamer and brambles
And a trail of black blood;
Blinding the pathways,
Choking the streams:
The White Worm slides in a dying nightmare,
The White Worm crawls through brackish water
And coils like a noose around the Tree of Dreams.

Burnt fruit and bitter
Hangs from broken branches,
Dangling half-bitten
Where there is no sun:
Stale and withered as a tale unspoken,
Tastes like ash on a stranger's tongue.

The White Worm winds where the silent trees
Crouch like twisted statues
In a street of disease;
In a city sick with secrets
Gripped by sullen frost,
Silhouettes and shadows of each life lost;
Where loveliness means nothing
While lonely creatures scream:
The White Worm crawls like a memory of laughter,
The White Worm slides through a sleep without Dreams.

In the crooked streets of the trembling town, babies wail and children complain as their mothers stir again the thin grim stew. And their fathers cannot mill the grain, their uncles cannot shear the sheep, their brothers cannot bring home meat, as the White Worm blackens every blade of grass on the common ground that surrounds the town.

And each sleepless night as they writhe in restless beds, no dreams from the Tree can soothe their heads. The wailing and the whispers, the moaning and the murmurs, the muttering and cursing all swell into a scream till the Great Men of the town open shuttered windows and listen as the mothers, the children and the fathers clatter through the narrow streets uttering one cry: "The White Worm must die. The White Worm must die!"

The Great Men in their ermine robes, their long gold chains and purple cloaks gather together in the town's Great Hall, gather together in conceit and pride, and lock the door on the people outside.

Outside the people shuffle and retreat.

"The Great Men know – they will have to decide how to defeat the Worm."

In the Great Hall the Great Men sit, wringing their hands and shuffling their feet. Swords and banners hang above, bloodstained in battles – now choked by the dust.

In the Great Hall the Great Men make speeches, blaming their fathers, blaming their sons, blaming each other for the curse of the Worm.

"Who will kill it?" the Great Men cry.

"The White Worm must die, the White Worm must die."

"Someone must do it – "

"Not I."

"Not I."

The Great Hall echoes as they all reply.

They gaze at the rusted weapons that hang about the roof.

"You cannot fight flames with a sword, as the White Worm flies in the dark night sky."

The Lord Mayor turns the key of the town's great treasure chest. He offers glinting diamonds; he offers glittering gold. But no-one in the Great Hall speaks a word.

The Lord Mayor listens to the knocking outside and slowly crosses the floor. He looks away from the crowd's pleading eyes when he finally opens the door.

"Your Great Men have considered and pondered long and hard. The Worm cannot be defeated by spear or by sword. We must find another answer – go back to your homes."

Back in her home in the smallest house at the darkest end of the narrowest street, the Shoemaker's Daughter rakes the grey ashes while she waits for her father's return. She remembers the pictures her eyes would create as she watched the flickering orange flames twist and dance in the grate.

"The only fire we ever see now is deep in the night when the White Worm flies and his vile breath lights up the sky. But that fire cannot comfort us; it cannot cook our food; it cannot melt metal to make nails for new boots; it cannot warm our home."

Her mother slowly closes the hollow cupboard's door and rattles the empty pans.

"The White Worm flies above, while we hide like scalded ants. But I hear your father coming – he'll tell us the Great Men's plans."

The Shoemaker shakes his head as he embraces his daughter and wife.

"No-one will fight the White Worm. No-one will risk his life. All the boots I have nailed, all the saddles I have stitched, all the jerkins of leather all put together are worthless if nobody has the pride to ride out and fight the Worm."

Night after night the Worm's cruel wings beat through the mournful air. Night after night he ransacks the town and takes what he wants to his lair.

As they cower in the cellar while the Shoemaker's Daughter cries, her mother spits through gritted teeth a twisted lullaby:

"The White Worm whispers,
The White Worm whines,
The White Worm slithers,
One coil at a time.

Where does the White Worm crawl to sleep?
      Deep in the dark earth,
      Hidden like a thief.
What does the White Worm claw and eat?
      Shadows and misery,
      Ashes and grief.

The White Worm drags through the dying wood,
      His dull heart beating
      Drums and blood:
Caskets of diamonds and sacks of gold;
      Pale fire sears the sky,
      Shivering and cold.

      Shadows and misery,
      Ashes and grief;
The White Worm whispers,
The White Worm whines.
      Drums and blood,
      Drums and blood;
The White Worm slithers
One coil at a time."

In the Great Hall the Great Men sit again, shaking their heads and shuffling their feet. In the Great Hall the Mayor makes a speech:

"The White Worm gets no pleasure from the treasure that he takes. We find fresh trails of treachery each morning when we wake. If you are all too cowardly to kill this Worm, we must offer him a sacrifice to stop him doing harm.

"Every night as the sun goes down – one of our daughters must leave this town. She must walk where the ground is scorched and bare, until she comes to the White Worm's lair."

The Great Men nod, and the Clerk takes down his words: "Better to lose one daughter each night than for the whole town to be burned."

Every night
One woman goes out
Across the burnt earth
Dead and black.

Daughter's tears
And Mother's grief
Knotted tight like a handkerchief;

She goes where the red sun
Chokes and bleeds,
Where grey leaves hang
From jagged trees.

At the edge of the dark wood
She stands and waits,
As smoke fills the sky
With a dull cloud of hate
Above the lair of the sleeping Worm.

The Shoemaker's Daughter cannot sleep. She follows the tracks of her stumbling feet through the shadowy, lifeless streets until she reaches the Great Hall's door.

The sky above her darkens once more as the White Worm swoops down silent and low. The Guard stands blindly shaking as if he's hypnotised, and the young girl slips behind him along the corridors inside, looking for a hiding place where she can lie and close her eyes.

The Shoemaker's Daughter sleeps a dreamless sleep. Suddenly she's woken by the tramp of urgent feet. Above her hang the banners, the shields and the swords. The Great Men stand all round her, and no-one says a word. The Lord Mayor fingers nervously his shining golden chain, as the Shoemaker's Daughter stares up at him, wide-eyed with a puzzled grin.

"Little girl," he says at last, "won't you tell me your name – and how you came to be here in this town's Great Hall, listening to talk and business that's no concern of yours at all?"

"I am the Shoemaker's Daughter," is all that she would say. "And if you do not know my name, then shame on you, for you see me every day.

"I crept in here to steal sweet sleep, since screams and wailing fill the streets of night with aching sound as the White Worm's wings beat overhead while he hovers round and round.

"But as I wake from my slumber, what is this I hear? You dress in furs and finery to try to hide your fear, but you Great Men, with all your schemes and lies, have decided nothing here.

"You are all too cowardly to go to meet the Worm – now you send good women out who never once return. I will not be a sacrifice like my sisters who have gone..."

"Stop, child. Do not think of it: you know you are too young."

"Then listen, Lord Mayor, and I'll tell you my plan, before it is my turn.

"Whatever we give the White Worm, he just wants more and more. He's ransacked all our silver. He's carried off our gold. He's stolen our songs and our dreaming and sucked our spirit dry. Now he just coils around our Tree, and waits for us to die.

"Let me talk to the White Worm. Let me be his friend. The White Worm can give us more alive than if we bring his life to an end.

"The White Worm can fly while we cower and hobble. The White Worm breathes fire while we sit and shiver. And if we fear the White Worm, so too must others. Let the White Worm defend us from enemies and strangers.

"Let me take a gift to him to show I mean no harm. A trinket from the treasure chest would work a soothing charm."

The Lord Mayor tightens hard his grip on the treasure chest's precious key. "All the town has left now is all that you can see. Why give any more to our enemy?"

The Shoemaker's Daughter answers the Mayor as she leaves the town's Great Hall:

"All the treasure I see glinting in that oaken chest – you took it from the people, my father and my mother. If you will give me nothing to take to greet the Worm, at least share it with the townsfolk to buy food and keep them warm."

But as the door of the Great Hall shuts solidly behind her, the Lord Mayor locks the treasure box and hides the key where no-one can find it.

The Shoemaker wakes early each morning, whether it's cloudy or bright to cut the leather, to shape the straps, to hammer the nails against his last; but today his daughter has woken before him.

While he sleeps, she washes her face. While he sleeps, she pulls on her dress. While he sleeps, she finds an empty basket and folds a cloth of clean, white linen to make a soft, warm lining. But the basket is empty. How can she fill it? She still has no gift to give to the Worm. The Shoemaker's Daughter gazes through the window at the dying dawn, flecked with red like the White Worm's fire.

She has no gold or silver because the Mayor refused her; and there's nothing left in her mother's cupboards but cobwebs and bitter dust. An empty basket is all she can take to make friends with the loathsome Worm.

As her father snores, she fastens her cloak and creeps like a shadow through the sad front door. Down heavy-eyed streets, where the townsfolk struggle through troubled sleep – waking to another hungry day with no dreams to help them on their way – the young girl hurries like a windblown leaf till she reaches the gates of the town.

Even the Gatekeeper sleeps at his post, worn out with watching the White Worm fly, circling and diving through the night's wild sky. Cunning as a magpie, the young girl steals his key; quickly and quietly she turns it in the lock; more slowly than the day's first waking yawn, the high gate opens wide.

Standing outside the town's gaunt walls, the Shoemaker's Daughter catches her breath. The rolling meadows where she used to play are black from the White Worm's fire. The pretty flowers that lined the way twist like brittle straw. The fields of wheat that stood so neat lie trampled, flattened and scorched.

And in the distance above the wood, above the clearing where the Tree of Dreams waits, a plume of grey smoke rises high into the air, thin as a ribbon of hate.

The Shoemaker's Daughter feels small and alone as she stands beneath the towering walls of the town, before setting off slowly beside the stream where the dull, sour water that used to run gaily turns sluggish and low between slime-covered stones.

Then out of a ditch he stumbles, totters, trips and tumbles, a bundle of grumbles and mumbles – the moon-eyed, mawkish Fool.

> "Lolloping and laughing,
> Yarroping and yawing,
> See me dancing dizzily
> Through singing village streets.
>
> My face is like a pancake
> And my belly's big and bloated,
> But I wear a yellow overcoat
> And I'm nimble on my feet.
>
> Children call me Rumble Tum
> As I gobble up a bag of plums,
> Then lie and suckle on my thumb
> Until I'm fast asleep.
>
> Giggling and gurgling,
> Capering and cawing,
> See me singing raucously
> Through sleepy village streets."

The Shoemaker's Daughter tries to run from the Fool, but he catches her hand then rolls into a ball.

"Where are you going to, my pretty girl?"

"I'm going to the Tree of Dreams to meet the cruel White Worm."

The Fool walks backwards in a zig-zag circle.

"First young lady, you must answer my riddle:

What's quiet as a whisper
And roars like thunder?

What escapes
When the joke is over?

What spreads like ripples
In a lake of water?"

The Shoemaker's Daughter breaks out into laughter. And as she laughs, the Fool laughs too:

"Laughter is the answer – catch it in your basket as quickly as you can. Let it keep you company on your journey to the Worm!"

She turns to wave to the tumbling Fool, but he's standing on one leg, fishing for thistledown out of the air to cover up his head.

The Shoemaker's smiling daughter follows the winding stream through the blackened fields towards the Tree of Dreams. She feels a hidden shadow shiver in the air and a thin voice whispering that speaks from nowhere:

> "When you look in the mirror
> You see me,
> But your eyes never quite meet my stare.
>
> From the moment you're born
> I am with you,
> A pale shadow that will always be there.
>
> When you sit down at night
> Don't you feel me
> Settled deep in your own favourite chair?
>
> I am your death.
> We'll embrace like old friends
> In that one sudden moment we share."

The Shoemaker's Daughter clutches her basket and gazes into the air.

"Where are you going to, lonely girl?" the grim Ghost asks as the dark mists swirl.

"I'm going to the Tree of Dreams to meet the terrible Worm."

The Ghost holds her fast in the empty meadow.

"First, brave child, you must answer my riddle:

> Today will quickly fade away
> As laughter wipes tears from sorrow,
> But come with me
> And you will see,
> When my hand turns the sand
> In the hourglass,
> Then yesterday becomes…"

"Tomorrow, grey spirit," says the Shoemaker's Daughter, "come back tomorrow and I'll have reasoned your answer."

"Today I need not fly away," the smiling Ghost replies, "because tomorrow is the answer I look for."

Careful not to lose the laughter given to her by the Fool, the young girl raises her basket's linen cloth as she stands at the edge of a bone dry pool.

As the grey Ghost's mist lifts and is gone, the Shoemaker's Daughter feels the warmth of the sun as it rises to the height of midday above the Tree of Dreams that still seems so far away.

Then a silent shadow surrounds her as if a cloud has stolen the sun. The Shoemaker's Daughter cries out loud, too afraid to run. Her frightened face stares upward, expecting to meet the Worm, but the ground shakes around her with the loudest voice she's ever heard:

"You have to walk round me.
You cannot pass through me.
I am the Giant
You never have seen;
I am the Giant –
But you see where I've been.

It's me
Who throws mountains and hills in your way,
Who swallows the sun at the end of the day;
It's me
Who rules alleys and streets where you play.

I am the Giant
You never have seen;
I am the Giant –
But you see where I've been.

It's me
Who builds city walls blocking your view:
I play hide-and-seek there
When I've nothing to do.

But no-one plays games
Trapped alone in their rooms;
Why don't they all know –
I'm just lonely too?"

"Don't cry, Giant," smiles the Shoemaker's Daughter, as his huge salty tears roll into the pool. The Giant looks so serious, the young girl starts to giggle.

"Wait, tiny creature, before you can leave me, first you must answer this riddle:

> You can feel it in my body,
> You can find it in my heart;
> It surges through my sinews
> To be ready when I start
> To walk a road of any length..."

"To work out this puzzle will take all my strength," the Shoemaker's Daughter replies.

"Strength is the answer – what a clever young wench: just open your basket and I'll breathe some inside."

Before she can thank him, the Giant walks away, crossing the hills with long, powerful strides.

So the Shoemaker's Daughter travels on, till at the bend of the winding track she knows there is no turning back, as she comes face to face with a Witching Woman, her warm eyes wild with wisdom.

"Once I shared the sleeping secrets
 Of creeping roots and echoing wells,
 The timeless music of the flowers
 And weeping shadows in the ditch;

 Then through the window of the future,
 I saw my Sisters taught the spells:
 Creating creatures caught in caskets
 By the twisting of a switch.

 My magic was my freedom
 From dark ponds and silent lanes,
 Till those who knew no better
 Dragged me screaming to their prison;

 But in my Sisters' shimmering caskets,
 The strangers glimpsed through silver frames
 Glared back like dead-eyed jailers
 From the blindness of my vision."

The Witching Woman dances beside the staring girl:

"I already know of your journey to the White Worm and the Tree; but before I'll let you go, you must answer me:

My first's in the moon
But not in the stars.

My second is kept
Bottled up in a jar.

My third is a gift
That you'll find in the ground.

My fourth you will sing
If you dance in a ring
Bearing ivy and incense
As you twist round and round.

My last creeps in with the black cat
And brings an end to logic…"

"To answer your riddle, I'll need all your magic," mutters the puzzled girl.

"Look no further, little one. You have found the clue. Put some magic in your basket, and I'll leave the rest to you."

Now the town seems far away, as the wood looms nearer, nearer. The young girl clutches her basket as her stomach knots in fear. Gorse and bracken tear at her dress as she enters the wood's dark shadows, when out of the shelter of a rambling bush steps a time-worn Gypsy Woman.

"You look weary, little one. Sit down while I sing you a song:

> When I was a girl
> I lived in the hill:
> I tore my cloak on a bramble thorn
> And sewed on a patch
> The colour of Dawn.
>
> When I was a girl
> I grew up and left home,
> But I tore my cloak on my mother's pin
> And sewed on a patch
> The colour of the Wind.
>
> When I was young
> I went from town to town
> With my cloak all torn from travelling enough:
> And I sewed on a patch
> The colour of Love.
>
> Now I am old,
> I will sing you a song
> Of the cloak that's wrapped round me
> All my days long.
> I'll show you a new patch
> Threaded through sharp as truth:
> I'll show you a new patch
> The colour of my Life."

The young girl runs her hands across the Gypsy's heavy cloak, but peers with a worried frown towards a plume of rising smoke.

"What brings you to the White Worm's wood?" the Gypsy Woman asks.

"The Worm has taken all we had, there's no food left in the town, no silver to buy what we need, no fire to keep us warm. Now the Great Men send one daughter each night to bribe the thankless Worm. I set out this morning to try to take their place. I want to meet the White Worm, to smile at his ugly face. I want the White Worm to listen to me, to stop plundering our helpless town and to free our Dreaming Tree.

"I wanted to bring a gift, to show I come as a friend, but the Lord Mayor locked the treasure box and said there was nothing to send. All I have is this empty basket that I'm carrying on my arm. I've collected nothing along the way to offer to the Worm."

The Gypsy Woman peers inside the young girl's basket.

"This basket looks empty. This basket feels full. You carry the strength of a Giant, the laughter of a Fool, the magic of a Witching Woman, and tomorrow's dawn-grey Ghost. Your basket is empty. Your basket is full. These are the gifts you will hang from the Tree. If

25

you hoard gold and silver you will only store up sorrow; but
Strength and Laughter and Magic will bring a new Tomorrow."
Then through the trees the young girl hears a whispering melody
rising to her ears, the song that is drenched in the townsfolk's fears.

"Every night
One woman goes out
Across the burnt earth
Dead and black:

Daughter's tears
And Mother's grief
Knotted tight like a handkerchief;

She goes where the red sun
Chokes and bleeds,
Where grey leaves hang
From jagged trees.

At the edge of the dark wood
She stands and waits,
As smoke fills the sky
With a dull cloud of hate
As she faces the terrible Worm."

But there's no ring of rotting bodies, no bleached and twisted bones, no empty grinning death's head skulls out under the watchful moon. Instead, in a clearing, a warm fire glows, and the voices of all the women she knows joined in a sisters' song.

"We've left the Great Men
  With their spears and swords,
  With their sullen promises
  And their worthless words.
  We've left them snoring
  Like lazy lords,
  And they know
  We'll never go home:
  We'll never go home,
  We'll never go home,
  They know we'll never go home."

Each woman greets the Shoemaker's Daughter as if she were their own. "Tell us, how is your mother – does she still scrimp and struggle? Tell us the toil and the trouble – tell us news of the town."

The young girl cannot hide her joy to see them all alive. "We thought the Worm would do his worst with the Great Men's sacrifice."

"The Great Men sent us one by one – but we live here together. While the White Worm sleeps all day, we weave dreams for the Tree, we sing and we play, under the wise wood's leafy roof that shelters us from the weather."

"Come and join us, youngest daughter. We do not need the Great Men, we do not fear the Worm. We have made our own life here; this is our new home."

The Shoemaker's Daughter listens and looks into their blissful eyes. The Shoemaker's Daughter listens, and thoughtfully replies:

"But I cannot forget the young ones, still living in the town. The White Worm will never let them sleep, and the Great Men will watch them famish and fade as they preen their flowing gowns.

"Now that I've reached my journey's end, I need to meet the White Worm to show we can be friends."

One bird sings in the clearing above the Tree of Dreams, as the Shoemaker's youngest daughter picks her way between the tangled thorns. She lifts the basket carefully to hang from the lowest branch. Light and lilting as the birdsong, she begins a circling dance:

"My basket is empty.
My basket is full."

The White Worm rises and opens wide his eyes. The White Worm uncoils and bares his poison fangs. The White Worm arches slowly and raises his scaly wings, as in a trembling voice the Shoemaker's Daughter sings:

"Look in my basket
At the gifts that I bring –

The Strength of a Giant,
The Laughter of a Fool,
The Magic of a Witching Woman
And Tomorrow's dawn-grey Ghost.

If you hoard gold and silver
You will only store up sorrow;
But Strength and Laughter and Magic
Will bring a new Tomorrow."

The White Worm listens. The White Worm sighs. The White Worm's fetid body slithers and unwinds. The White Worm casts a jaundiced eye at his pile of tawdry treasure.

"You can steal me all the gold in the world. You can bring me all the silver. But as each bauble starts to tarnish, it's just a lump of metal. This basket you have brought me is worth more than anyone can measure. Tomorrow, with the Strength of Magic and Laughter, we'll build a new home together."

29

He takes the Shoemaker's Daughter on his scarred and blistered back, and leads the waiting women down the charred and winding track. Across the blackened common, the scorched and wasted plain, the White Worm leads them all to the gates of the town again and cries out to the Great Men cowering inside:

> "I can give you fire to warm you,
>   I can fill your homes with light,
>   And as my wings beat pale and silent
>   Above your rooftops every night,
>   I can bring you a dream –
>   A dream from the Tree,
>   But all your dreams will be worthless
>   Until you see
>   That the only way your town can ever be set free
>   Is when you walk from your Great Hall
>   Into streets you dare not name,
>   Gaze through doorways of despair
>   Choked with poverty and shame:
>   Hopes and dreams are meaningless
>   Until you begin to care;
>   Silver and gold worth less than nothing,
>   Until you break the lock
>   Of your treasure box
>   And learn to love..."

" – and share," concludes the Lord Mayor, wisely shaking his head. He has listened long and carefully to all the White Worm said. The treasure box is opened, and the Great Men take off their gowns as they divide the contents equally among the people of the town.

The Shoemaker's Daughter runs through the streets to greet her father and mother. There's a great commotion in every house as neighbours call to each other: "Pass the ladle, sift the grain, lend me, please, some flour." Smiles return to sad faces again, and a feast is cooked in an hour; packed and stored in hampers while children sing with glee: and grandparents, sisters and lovers lead the way to the Tree of Dreams.

The tall Tree gathers each family back to its beating heart, releasing their shimmering, pent-up dreams out into the gathering dark. Then as the colours touch them, the creatures return to their home: the blackbirds and thrushes, linnets and robins singing as if they were one.

"While the White Worm circles high
    To see they meet no harm,
    Over the hills so far away
    A mawkish Fool and a shadowy Ghost
    Join a gangling Giant at play
    As they dance a Witching Woman's waltz
    Along the Gypsy's winding way
    Till the full moon rises silently
    To light a smiling lullaby
    Above the Tree of Dreams."